A JOYOUS DE WOLFE CHRISTMAS

A MEDIEVAL SHORT STORY

BY KATHRYN LE VEQUE

KATHRYN LE VEQUE NOVELS

Medieval Romance:

The de Russe Legacy:
The White Lord of Wellesbourne
The Dark One: Dark Knight
Beast
Lord of War: Black Angel
The Iron Knight

The de Lohr Dynasty:
While Angels Slept (Lords of East
Anglia)
Rise of the Defender
Steelheart
Spectre of the Sword
Archangel
Unending Love
Shadowmoor
Silversword

Great Lords of le Bec:
Great Protector
To the Lady Born (House of de
Royans)
Lord of Winter (Lords of de Royans)

Lords of Eire:
The Darkland (Master Knights of
Connaught)
Black Sword
Echoes of Ancient Dreams (time
travel)

De Wolfe Pack Series:
The Wolfe
Serpent
Scorpion (Saxon Lords of Hage – Also
related to The Questing)
The Lion of the North
Walls of Babylon

Dark Destroyer
Nighthawk
Warwolfe
ShadowWolfe
DarkWolfe
A Joyous de Wolfe Christmas

Ancient Kings of Anglecynn:
The Whispering Night
Netherworld

Battle Lords of de Velt:
The Dark Lord
Devil's Dominion

Reign of the House of de Winter:
Lespada
Swords and Shields (also related to The
Questing, While Angels Slept)

De Reyne Domination:
Guardian of Darkness
The Fallen One (part of Dragonblade
Series)
With Dreams Only of You

**Unrelated characters or family
groups:**
The Gorgon (Also related to Lords of
Thunder)
The Warrior Poet (St. John and de
Gare)
Tender is the Knight (House of d'Vant)
Lord of Light
The Questing (related to The Dark
Lord, Scorpion)
The Legend (House of Summerlin)

**The Dragonblade Series: (Great
Marcher Lords of de Lara)**
Dragonblade

Island of Glass (House of St. Hever)
The Savage Curtain (Lords of Pembury)
The Fallen One (De Reyne Domination)
Fragments of Grace (House of St. Hever)
Lord of the Shadows
Queen of Lost Stars (House of St. Hever)

Lords of Thunder: The de Shera Brotherhood Trilogy
The Thunder Lord
The Thunder Warrior
The Thunder Knight

The Great Knights of de Moray:
Shield of Kronos

Highland Warriors of Munro:
The Red Lion
Deep Into Darkness

The House of Ashbourne:
Upon a Midnight Dream

The House of D'Aurilliac:
Valiant Chaos

The House of De Nerra:
The Falls of Erith
Vestiges of Valor

The House of De Dere:
Of Love and Legend

Time Travel Romance: (Saxon Lords of Hage)
The Crusader
Kingdom Come

<u>**Contemporary Romance:**</u>

Kathlyn Trent/Marcus Burton Series:
Valley of the Shadow
The Eden Factor
Canyon of the Sphinx

The American Heroes Series:
The Lucius Robe
Fires of Autumn
Evenshade
Sea of Dreams
Purgatory

Other Contemporary Romance:
Lady of Heaven
Darkling, I Listen
In the Dreaming Hour

Sons of Poseidon:
The Immortal Sea

Pirates of Britannia Series (with Eliza Knight):
Lady of the Moon
Savage of the Sea
Leader of Titans

<u>**Multi-author Collections/Anthologies:**</u>
Sirens of the Northern Seas (Viking romance)

Note: All Kathryn's novels are designed to be read as stand-alones, although many have cross-over characters or cross-over family groups. Novels that are grouped together have related characters or family groups.

Series are clearly marked. All series contain the same characters or family groups except the American Heroes Series, which is an anthology with unrelated characters.

There is NO particular chronological order for any of the novels because they can all be read as stand-alones, even the series.

For more information, find it in **A Reader's Guide to the Medieval World of Le Veque.**

TABLE OF CONTENTS

AUTHOR'S NOTE

I have had so many readers ask me "when will Scott and Troy come together again?". Considering I don't have any more "Sons of de Wolfe" novels planned for the near future, I didn't want readers to have to wait until I decided to incorporate that into a later novel. Therefore, A DE WOLFE JOYOUS CHRISTMAS was born.

The short story (and it is short!) revolves around the return of the de Wolfe Prodigal Son, Scott de Wolfe, but also featured heavily in it is James de Wolfe. If you recall your de Wolfe history, James will die in 1282 in Wales, and even I don't think I can resurrect the man (although never say never). This story is also a tribute to James and we get a brief glimpse into his life, but it's increasingly difficult for me to write about James, considering what happens to him in the future. Had I known I was going to become so attached to him when he was first mentioned in SERPENT, I may not have let the man fall victim to the Welsh. As Penelope says in SERPENT, "James died in Papa's arms..." and knowing how attached William is to his children, I'm not even sure I could write that scene without copious amounts of ugly crying.

But... life goes on, as you'll see within this short Christmas story. It's to satisfy those of you who have wanted to see Scott and Troy together again, something that was bound to be somewhat of a miracle.

So, enjoy the tale. I enjoyed, very much, writing it.

The happiest of holidays from me to you,
Kathryn

THE NEXT GENERATION WOLFE PACK

The Wolfe

William and Jordan Scott de Wolfe

Scott (married to Lady Athena de Norville, issue)

Troy (married to Lady Helene de Norville, has issue)

Patrick (married to Lady Brighton de Favereux, has issue)

James – Killed in Wales June 1282 (married to Lady Rose Hage, has issue)

Katheryn (James' twin) Married Sir Alec Hage, has issue

Evelyn (married to Sir Hector de Norville, has issue)

Baby de Wolfe – died same day. Christened Madeleine.

Edward (married to Lady Cassiopeia de Norville, has issue)

Thomas

Penelope (married to Bhrodi de Shera, has issue)

Kieran and Jemma Scott Hage

Mary Alys (adopted) married, with issue

Baby Hage, died same day. Christened Bridget.

Alec (married to Lady Katheryn de Wolfe, has issue)

Christian (died Holy Land 1269 A.D.) no issue

Moira (married to Sir Apollo de Norville, has issue)

Kevin (married to Annavieve de Ferrers, has issue)

Rose (widow of Sir James de Wolfe, has issue)

Nathaniel

Paris and Caladora Scott de Norville

Hector (married to Lady Evelyn de Wolfe, has issue)

Apollo (married to Lady Moira Hage, has issue)

Helene (married to Sir Troy de Wolfe, has issue)

Athena (married to Sir Scott de Wolfe, has issue)

Adonis

Cassiopeia (married to Sir Edward de Wolfe, has issue)

PART ONE

BRIGHT WINTER SKIES

Christmas, 1274 A.D.

The de Wolfe stronghold of Castle Questing

THE SNOWS WERE fierce along the borders this year. The first snow of the season hitting about a week before Christmas and possibly dumping an entire year's worth of snow onto the countryside in just a few days. The beauty of it was that the entire land was white, from the trees to the structures to the meadows – a pristine, pure white that, under bright winter skies, was blindingly brilliant. But the dreary of it, if there was such a thing, was that there had only been one pristine white day in the past week, and it happened to be Christmas Day. On that day, the inhabitants of Castle Questing had emerged from the keep for a day of celebration in the snow.

The first one bolting from the entry to Questing's keep was

eight-year-old Penelope de Wolfe. With her dark braided hair trailing behind her, she dashed out into the snowy bailey and headed towards the gatehouse, while her nieces and nephews and cousins ran out behind her. With children screaming and frolicking under bright blue skies, the day promised to be, at the very least, a noisy one.

Truthfully, the days past when the snow was billowing out of the sky had already been noisy and crowded inside the walls of Castle Questing. It was a big keep and could easily house dozens of people, but it was at capacity. A wedding was to take place on Christmas Day and not only had the groom's family come to Questing, but all of the de Wolfe extended family were in attendance as well. Even though some of the families weren't connected to the de Wolfe household by marriage or by blood, they were headed by men who had served the head of the House of de Wolfe – William – in some capacity over the years, and had faced life and death with the man, so they were therefore considered family.

It was a grand gathering, indeed.

This included the houses of de Bocage, Ellsrod, Gray, de Fortlage, de Longley, and Payton-Forrester. More had been invited for this festive occasion, but those were the only families who could make it before the snows hit. With such heavy snow on the ground, they were all bound to their locations, meaning that travel in the north was difficult if not impossible.

For the coming wedding, which would take place at sunset

on this very eve, several of the younger knights had set out for Kelso Abbey to bring a priest back to Questing to perform the wedding mass. William de Wolfe and his Scottish wife, Jordan, were great benefactors of Kelso, so the monks had been more than willing to perform whatever religious ceremonies needed by de Wolfe. Troy de Wolfe, along with his brother, Patrick, brothers Hector and Adonis de Norville, and cousin Alec Hage had set out for Kelso the day before, during a snowy downpour, to bring the priest back to Questing. Although Kelso was a mere ten miles from the de Wolfe seat, in weather such as this, even a simple trip was an effort.

Therefore, it was the mothers of the young men who waited nervously for them to return – Lady Jordan along with her cousin, Jemma, mother to the Hage knight, and another cousin, Caladora, who was mother to the de Norville brothers – were crowded in Jordan's solar, which was right at the front of Questing's keep near the entry door, and gave them perfect views over the bailey and gatehouse. From there, they could see everything, including the children and husbands frolicking in the pristine snow outside. When the snowballs began to fly in the bailey, Jemma, who was seated next to the window, shook her head in resignation.

"Now, it begins," she said. "They're already doing battle outside. They'll pick sides and before we know it, we'll have freezing bairns who have been pummeled with snowballs."

Jordan was sitting next to her cousin, sewing on a heavy winter tunic for her husband, but she put the sewing in her lap and peered from the window at her cousin's comment.

"We canna stop them," she said in resignation. "The lot of them have been caged up in Questing since the snows started. Now they'll beat each other tae death with snowballs and we canna stop it."

A flicker of a grin crossed Jemma's lips. "Ah," she said with satisfaction, as she had spied something out in the bailey. "Now, *that* was worth waiting for. It seems that Rosie has hit her Uncle Paris in the face with a snowball. Good for ye, lass!"

She yelled the last four words out of the window, causing Jordan to grin and pass a glance at her cousin, Caladora, who was Paris' wife. Tall, slender, and red-haired, Caladora was a truly gentle and kind creature, but she was fiercely protective over her proud and sometimes arrogant husband. In fact, in years past, Caladora had been known to slap Jemma over what she considered Jemma's unreasonable hatred of Paris, but the truth was that Paris and Jemma went back many, many years. They knew each other very well and had a love/hate relationship as a brother and sister would. Paris taunted, Jemma reacted, and all the world was right when those two were name-calling. Only Caladora didn't see it that way; she thought her cousin Jemma was rather nasty at times.

"Rosie is tae be a bride in a few hours," Caladora calmly pointed out as she sewed on a small garment for one of her grandchildren. "Do ye think she should be outside at all?"

Jemma was grinning boldly now as she watched from the window as her youngest daughter, Rose, charged her Uncle

Paris and sent the man tripping back into the snow. Rose was much like Jemma in that she was tiny, pretty, and very spirited. It was like watching Jemma when she had been a young girl, which was probably why Paris seemed to gravitate towards Rose. Not only did he have the mother to taunt, but now the daughter as well.

But she loved every minute of it.

"Let the lass have some fun," Jemma finally said, glad that Caladora couldn't see what a pummeling her husband was receiving. "Soon enough, she'll be expected tae behave as a wife. She's only seen eighteen years; let her be young a moment longer."

Jordan glanced at Jemma, hearing a wistfulness in her tone. "Ye know that James will make her a fine husband," she assured Jemma softly. "Ye know my lad. He's the kindest lad of the bunch and he loves Rosie. He'll not curb her spirit."

Jemma's smile faded as she watched her daughter, now throwing a snowball at her future husband. "Nay," she said after a moment. "He'll not. If ever there was a man made for Rosie, 'tis James. He reminds me much of Kieran with his gentle ways. I couldna ask for a better husband for my lass."

There was sadness in her voice as she spoke, the worry of a wife in love with a man who wasn't doing so well as of late. Jordan smiled up at her cousin, grasping the woman by the arm in a supportive gesture when she spoke of her husband. Kieran Hage was the gentle giant among them; he and Paris were William's very best friends, a bond between them that was closer than brothers.

Whereas Paris was a proud extrovert, Kieran tended to be quiet and more of an introvert. But there was no one fiercer in battle and Kieran's strength was unmatched. Yet, he hadn't been feeling well over the past year and the physic said that it was his heart, a diagnosis that had greatly affected Jemma. She loved her husband with every fiber of her being, a man she could not live without, and his health issue had been a devastating one to them all.

That was why this day was so important to the Hage family as well as the de Wolfe family; it would see two of their children bonded in marriage, a bright spot in a rather dismal year. Even now, Jemma could see Kieran out in the snow, being hit by snowballs by some rowdy children, and then firing back snowballs that ended up hitting Penelope in the side of the head, getting snow in her ear.

As Penelope burst into tears, Uncle Kieran was at her side, soothing her and helping her pick snow out of her ear. Jemma knew the man would suffer unimaginable guilt for the rest of the day for hitting Penelope in the ear with a well-aimed snowball. He was just that sensitive.

"I hear Penny wailing," Jordan said, setting her sewing down completely and peering from the window to see her daughter crying with Kieran at her side. "What happened tae my lass this time?"

This time. Penelope de Wolfe, a very late baby for her mother and father, and the youngest de Wolfe child, was also the child who ruled the roost. Her parents doted on her, and she was a bright and beautiful girl. But she was also terribly spoiled, and anything that didn't go her way usually resulted in tears or a tantrum. Jordan had long learned not to run to her daughter's side every time the girl made a sound, but her husband hadn't yet developed that restraint. Even with Kieran at Penelope's side, William pulled himself away from his grandchildren to see what had Penelope so upset. Jordan shook her head in resignation.

"The lass will never learn tae stand for herself if William runs tae her every time she utters a peep." Jordan sighed, sitting down and collecting her sewing again. "I fear for the day she marries; I truly do. I am not sure what William will do when he canna have her by his side, always."

Caladora looked up from her sewing. "He clings tae all of his children these days," she said quietly. "It is not simply Penelope."

"What do ye mean?"

Caladora didn't say anything for a moment because it was something they all knew, something not readily spoke of. "Because of Scott."

Jordan's pleasant mood sank at the mention of the son she'd not seen in years. Even the mention of his name brought a lump to her throat, but she fought it. Today was a joyful day and she wouldn't let thoughts of her absent son spoil that.

"William has made amends with Scott," she said quietly. "He's gone tae Castle Canaan where Scott is in command and he's spoken tae him. They've said what needed tae be said."

Caladora looked at her. "But what about ye? Have ye yet said what needed tae be said tae him?"

It was a familiar argument and Jordan turned back to her sewing. "Ye know I havena," she said. "I've not seen my son since he left Questing those years ago."

"Will ye go and see him, then?"

She shook her head. "Nay," she said. "He knows where I am. If he wants tae make amends with me, then he'll come. 'Tis not for me to seek him out."

Caladora had heard that attitude before and she didn't like it; it irked her. "At least ye still have yer sons, Jordie," she said. "At least ye can go tae him. I canna say that I still have my daughters, but if I did, no matter how far away from me they were, I wouldna let any more time pass without seeing them again. If something happens tae Scott tomorrow, ye'd be miserable the rest of yer life."

At the window, Jemma glanced at the pair as they skimmed the surface of a volatile conversation. It was such a sad situation, truly, something that affected all of them so deeply. It was a situation that had started four years ago when the eldest sons of William and Jordan, twins Scott and Troy, had both lost their wives and several of their children in a terrible drowning accident.

Compounding the issue was that the wives had been two of Paris and Caladora's daughters. The women and their younger children, four in all, had been traveling by coach to Berwick when a bridge gave way and dumped all of them into a swollen river. Both wives and all four children had perished, leaving devastation of two families in their wake.

It had been a terrible time for all concerned.

As Paris and Caladora had lost themselves in their grief, Scott and Troy had each dealt with their loss quite different. Troy had thrown himself into battle, into his duties, anything to work through the pain of losing his wife and two youngest children, while Scott had simply run away. That was the last he'd see of Questing and of his entire family, save his father.

William had kept track of his son no matter where the man had gone. William had even written to the king for assistance with Scott. Rather than see the man wander aimlessly, which he did for the first year, the king had given him a command at a strategic castle in Cumbria. Scott had settled in and eventually married the widow of the man who used to command the castle. When William heard of the marriage, he'd gone to see Scott and old wounds were healed. But Jordan was correct; Scott had remained away from Questing, and all of the memories there, since the day he'd left.

She wondered if she would ever see him again.

But at least her loss wasn't what Caladora's had been. The woman had lost two of her beloved daughters and Jordan knew that hers was the greater loss. But sometimes, Jordan felt Scott's absence as painfully as if he had died.

In a sense, the old Scott had.

"I know, lass," Jordan said after a moment, reaching out to

lay a hand on her cousin's arm as she reflected on the past four years. "What ye've suffered is beyond all human endurance. I dinna mean tae compare yer loss tae mine. But sometimes... sometimes I feel as if Scott has died. He's not the same man, my sweet and funny lad. I havena seen him in years. I fear that he will never return tae Questing. Too many terrible memories for him. Sometime I wonder if I am part of those terrible memories."

Caladora clasped Jordan's hand, squeezing it tightly. As women, they suffered in silence sometimes. It was their job to be stronger than the rest, to show courage and fortitude in situations that would crumble others. But among themselves, they could let their guards down. Jordan squeezed Caladora's hand in return, her focus turning to her pale cousin.

"How *are* ye, lass?" she asked her cousin softly. "We've not spoken of Athena and Helene in some time."

Caladora sighed faintly. "I have days when I feel as if everything is so dark, that I canna get out of bed," she admitted. "But Paris... he dunna think I know but, sometimes, I hear him weeping. Whenever he sees the older children of Helene and Athena, he weeps. I think he still feels as if he's failed his daughters. He thinks he should have been there tae save them."

It was a painful admission of a parent's guilt. Jordan understood it well. "William has spoken tae me of his regrets," she said. "When he sees Scott's older lads, Will and Tommy, and Troy's son, Andreas, he regrets that they lost their mothers at such a young age. I believe he, too, feels guilt that he wasna there tae save them."

Hushed words spoken about a terrible tragedy. Before the mood grew too dark and painful, Jordan took a deep breath and picked up her sewing.

"So, we remember Athena and Helene and the children tonight," she said with renewed fortitude. "We remember them at the marriage so that even in spirit, they are with us."

Caladora simply nodded, not feeling particularly enthusiastic now that memories of her dead daughters and grandchildren were heavy on her mind. But Jemma, who had been watching the exchange, came away from the window, her focus on her cousins.

"Of course they are with us," she said. "Callie, I dinna tell ye because I wanted it tae be a surprise, but Rosie's wedding dress has ribbon on it that was on Athena's wedding dress. It also has a sash that I took from Helene's dress. Paris gave them tae me. I wanted tae honor the lasses in such a way. I hope ye dunna mind."

Caladora's head came up, her blue eyes brimming with tears. "'Tis a beautiful thought, Jemma," she said sincerely. "I dunna mind at all."

Jemma went to her cousin and gave the woman a squeeze. "Rosie is most excited for the ceremony tonight and tae show ye her dress," she said. "Act surprised when she tells ye. She wanted tae surprise ye, too."

Caladora sniffled, flicking away the tears that threatened. "I'll act surprised," she said. "I might even give her a good cry. Do ye think she'll like that?"

Jemma grinned. "She'll love it," she said. Then, she moved

back over to the window where the snowball fight was starting to dwindle. "Looks as if Penny has come inside, Jordie. Ye may want tae see tae her ear."

Jordan set her sewing aside yet again and rose from her seat. "I dunna know why I should go," she said. "William is probably doing all the mothering tae the lass that she'll ever need."

Jemma grinned. "I dunna see William out in the yard, either."

Jordan snorted. "See? What did I tell ye." She sighed heavily and headed for the door. "Mayhap, I'd better go see tae my lass. Her da's sympathy only goes so far sometimes."

As the woman headed from the solar, Jemma and Caladora were smiling, each woman settling back to her sewing. It wasn't just William who doted on his children; Paris and Kieran did enough of it, too. After Penelope was born, Kieran had even hinted at wanting to have another child, but Jemma wouldn't hear of it; with six children already, her childbearing days were over, much to her husband's disappointment.

But Jemma had to admit... sometimes, she wished she'd had just one more child. Watching William with Penelope had given her that longing. After all, Kieran deserved a lass to spoil and dote on, too. What was one more spoiled half-Scottish lass to rule the roost at Questing?

Jemma grinned at the mental image, something she could only wonder about now.

But it would have been fun to see.

PART TWO

HIS ROSE

TALL, HANDSOME, BLOND, and blue-eyed, James de Wolfe was in the stableyard on this bright winter's day, watching a groom lead a very young Belgian warmblood around the yard. This was his new horse, one he intended to train for battle, because the beast came from fine bloodlines and was strong and spirited. But the stablemaster thought the horse had a bad hip because of the way he tended to stand, so James was watching the horse as it was walked around the yard, listening to the stablemaster tell him why the horse's gait was odd.

It wasn't exactly the type of activity a groom should be doing only a few hours before his wedding, but James wasn't even sure he would be married today considering how heavy the snow was. The roads were piled high with the stuff, making it very difficult to travel, and his brothers had departed for Kelso yesterday and still hadn't returned. A trip like that normally took a morning to complete, there and back. Therefore, James wasn't entirely sure when the marriage would take place. Spending time in the stable was simply a way of burning off his anxiety.

He was rather eager to marry his Rose.

As he stood there and watched the horse walk by, Kevin Hage and Andreas de Wolfe entered the stableyard and demanded their horses. Big, muscular Kevin was James' cousin while Andreas was his nephew, eldest son of his brother, Troy.

James merely waved at the pair as they collected their horses and raced off just as William entered the yard. He then glanced over at his father, wrapped up in heavy tunics and a woolen cloak that, as he came closer, appeared to be soaking wet. James frowned.

"Why are you all wet?" he asked the man. "You'd better take that cloak off before Mother sees you. After the lung sickness you had last year, you should know better."

William simply grinned at his son; the man was still tall, dark, and handsome, even in his advancing years, and he was still powerful enough that most men couldn't best him in battle. The legendary Wolfe of the Border was still a force to be reckoned with, except when it came to his wife. She was the one force that could overpower his own, so he took his son's statement seriously.

"We were playing in the snow," he said. "By the way – Rosie can throw a snowball that can disable a grown man, so I would be careful if I were you should she throw anything at you."

James chuckled. "She already has," he said. "I am fast enough to dodge it, fortunately."

William's eyebrows lifted. "Do you mean to say you are making the woman angry enough to throw something at you and you aren't even married yet?"

James began to laugh; it was one of his personality traits, this impish laugh that would easily come over him.

"It takes very little to make her angry," he said. "She is much like her mother in that respect, but I have learned well from Uncle Kieran. He tells me that the angrier she becomes, the more groveling I must do."

"Is that so?"

"It is. He also says to spank her when all else fails."

Now, William started to chuckle. "He is a very wise man," he said. "And speaking of wise men, I came to tell you that we believe your brothers have been sighted in the distance. With the clearness of the day, they are still a mile or so out, but we can easily see them against the white landscape. We are watching the approach now."

James felt both relief and excitement at that statement. "So they made it, did they?" he said. "I was coming to wonder if they would."

William nodded, seeing the pleasure in his son's face. It was sweet, really; James was very much in love with the spirited Rose, a love story they'd all watched unfold for the past two years, ever since Rose began to blossom into a woman and grew past the phase where she would rather punch a boy than be nice to him.

James was several years older than Rose was and only knew her as that rough-and-tumble little girl, but when she'd hit her sixteenth birthday, something changed – suddenly, rough-and-tumble Rosie became curvaceous, beautiful Rosie and James wasn't blind to the fact. A sweet romance had blossomed from the seeds of friendship and, now, Rose and James were about to embark on their married lives together.

William couldn't have been happier.

"You were not the only one questioning whether or not they would arrive," he said to his son. "Kieran and some of the others were talking about heading out to find them."

James shook his head. "Uncle Kieran should not be exerting himself like that," he said. "You know what the physic said."

William sobered dramatically; he didn't like to be reminded of his dearest friend's health problem. "I do," he said. "Luckily, we do not have to worry about him overextending himself. But… there is something I want to say to you before your brothers arrive with the priest. After that, I fear I might not have another chance before Rosie takes you away from me."

James turned to his father, a smile playing on his lips. "What about, Papa?" he asked. "The ways of men and women? You are too late. I already know what I am supposed to do on my wedding night."

William chuckled. "Bloody hell, who told you? Was it Paris? Whatever he told you is a lie. Women do not like to be tied down and spanked."

James couldn't stop laughing. "That is *not* what he told me they liked."

"What was it, then?"

"If I tell you, you will only punch him."

"I may punch him still. What did he tell you, James?"

James knew the two older knights would go at it, genuinely, if William was mad enough, so he put his hands on his father to calm the man down. "He only told me to be patient," he said. "I swear it. Now, what did you want to tell me, Papa?"

William looked at his son; he was his fourth son, the twin to his first daughter, Katheryn. When the pair had been born, James had struggled for his first few weeks, fighting to live. He didn't eat well and slept constantly, and William remembered the very real fear of losing his child. But the infant had lived and, eventually, thrived. Today, he was one of the finest and most powerful knights the north had ever seen.

But it was more than that for William – James didn't have the fiery passion about battle and warfare that his older three had. Scott, Troy, and Patrick were the consummate knights, living and breathing battle. James could match any of his brothers' prowess in a fight, but he had something more that they didn't – compassion for the enemy, a deep compassion that, at times, had turned him into a brooding and moody man. James felt more deeply than most, was more patient than Job himself, and would much rather negotiate his way out of a fight than quickly draw arms. They were such wonderful qualities and William adored his boy for them. He had a soft spot for

James and his wise, gentle ways.

What did he want to tell him? Gazing into his handsome face, there were so many things that came to mind. He'd had to have this same talk with Scott, Troy, and Patrick before their weddings but, somehow with James, it was different. He just wanted to hug the man and hold him close. After a moment, he put a hand on his son's shoulder.

"I wanted to tell you how proud I am of the man you have become," he said, suddenly feeling a lump in his throat where, moments before, there had been laughter. "After today, you will go forth to become the head of your own family, and I want to tell you how proud I am of you. I have watched a skinny, pale young man with a silly giggle grow into a man of such character and strength. It has been a privilege watching you become the man I see before me, James. I wanted you to know that."

James hasn't expected those words from his father. In fact, he began to tear up and, by the time William was finished, he threw his arms around his father's neck and hugged him tightly. For a moment, he simply couldn't speak.

"I love you, Da," he said hoarsely. "You are the greatest man I have ever known, the man I most wish to emulate. Know that I will do my best to always be like you and to always honor you and the de Wolfe name. I shall not fail, I swear it, nor will any of my sons. We will all make you proud."

He released his father and saw that William was wiping away his own tears. William cupped James' head in his big hands, gazing deep into those sky-blue eyes. He'd always joked with his wife about James' coloring, a blond-haired, blue-eyed child in a family full of dark-haired people. He would tease Jordan and tell her that James must have been fathered by a passing Viking, but the truth was that James' features mirrored William's. He looked very much like his father. William kissed his son on the cheek and forced a smile as he dropped his hands.

"There is nothing you could do to dishonor the de Wolfe name," he said. "You are my son and I shall always be proud of you. Now, as for your wedding night, I am afraid that I can only tell you what Paris has told you – to be patient, be kind, and be understanding. Rosie is much like her mother in that she is rather highly-strung, so you are simply going to have to be as kind and gentle as you can be."

James' grin returned. "That is exactly what Uncle Kieran said," he said. Then, he hesitated a moment before continuing. "Besides... I am not entirely sure if I should tell you this, but Rosie will *not* be nervous."

He was looking at his father rather knowingly and William understood the implication immediately. William fought off a grin at his rather naughty and amorous son.

"Whatever you do, do not tell your Uncle Kieran that," he grunted. "She is his daughter, after all. Up until you marry her, it is still his duty to defend her honor and I am not entirely sure you would survive his wrath."

James' laughter returned. "I did not tell you simply to boast,

Da," he said. "I told you that for a reason. In seven months, when Rosie gives birth to my son, I will have to ask you to intercede on my behalf with Uncle Kieran. That may be the wrath you are speaking of."

William's eyes widened. "She... she is with child, lad?"

"She is."

William's jaw dropped. At first, he was genuinely shocked. But after a split-second, he threw his arms around his son and hugged the man tightly.

"That is the greatest gift I could receive this Christmas season," he said, releasing the grinning man. "I am genuinely thrilled, James. May I tell your mother?"

James shook his head. "Nay, for she will tell Aunt Jemma, and Aunt Jemma will tell Kieran," he said. "I do not wish to defend myself from him until it is absolutely necessary."

William understood. "It will be difficult to keep that secret, but I shall honor your wishes," he said. But he was quite elated about it. "Mayhap you should put your horse away and we will go into the bailey and stop your future wife from exerting herself. She is carrying a de Wolfe heir, after all."

James grabbed hold of his father as the man turned for the bailey. "Nay, Da," he said. "If you try to stop her from playing, she'll know I have told you, and then I will have to defend myself from her. That is not something I wish to do on my wedding night."

William relented. "Very well," he said. "I will not say a word, but I must leave you now and find Penelope. Kieran hit her in the head with a snowball and got snow in her ear. She swears she is going to die from it."

James simply shook his head at his overprotective father, at least when it came to Penelope. Everyone knew how the man coddled her. Therefore, James waved the man on just as Rose entered the stableyard in search of her betrothed. James was certain from the way his father hugged Rose that the woman would suspect that William knew of their little secret, but she didn't seem suspicious. She seemed very touched by his display of affection. As William left the yard, Rose turned to James.

"What is the matter with your father today?" she asked. "He seems very emotional."

James smiled at her. "Of course he is emotional," he said. "His favorite son is marrying. Why shouldn't he be emotional?"

Rose laughed softly, looking very much like her mother in that action. Petite, with big breasts, Rose Elizabeth Scott Hage was a vibrant and lovely woman with dark hair, pale skin, and delicate features. She had a smile that lit up the heavens as far as James was concerned.

"I suppose I understand," she said. "My father is the same way. He cannot look at me and not get teary-eyed today."

Reaching out, James put his arms around Rose, pulling her up against him. She felt warm and soft in his arms, a contentment that filled him like nothing else. *His* Rose.

"I have heard, from no one in particular, that you are throwing snowballs quite viciously," he said.

Rose wrapped her arms around his waist, her strong young

knight. "Who is telling such lies?"

"I said it was no one in particular."

Her eyes narrowed at him. "It was your father, wasn't it? He told you because I hit Penelope twice, rather hard."

"She deserved it."

"She hit me in the face."

James chuckled. "The nasty wench! Shall I punish her for you?"

Rose hugged him tightly, giggling. "You would have to go through your father to do that, and he would not acquiesce easily," she said. "Nay, leave it be. I will get Penelope someday when she least expects it."

"Do not forget that she knows how to use a sword."

"So do I."

James laughed at the mental image. "Now, *that* is some-thing I would pay money to see. That shall be great entertainment, watching you two face off."

"I shall win, too."

"Of that, I have no doubt," he said, giving her a squeeze and a kiss.

The stable boy came around yet again, leading a horse James was no longer looking at, and he motioned for the boy to return the horse to his stall. When the lad moved to take the fat, lazy horse back to its food and bedding, James took Rose by the hand and began to lead her out of the stableyard.

"I have heard that my brothers have been sighted," he told her. "Did you hear that, also?"

Rose nodded, clutching his hand tightly. "I did," she said. "Some of the younger men ran out to meet them; Kevin and Andreas, in fact."

She was speaking of her brother, Kevin Hage, and of Troy's eldest teenage son, Andreas. James nodded.

"I saw them take their horses," he said. "I did not realize where they were going."

Rose squeezed his hand. "Are you nervous?"

He looked at her, frowning. "What about?"

She grinned that toothy grin. "Marrying me," she said. "You cannot refuse, you know. If you do, I will tell my father that you ravaged me and forced me to bear your child."

His eyes flew up in mock outrage. "You wicked minx," he said. "Would you really tell him that?"

"Aye."

"Then know I am not afraid of your father. Well, not much."

"Shall we tell him our secret now, then?"

James grunted. "Hell, no," he said. "I do not want to be bruised and bleeding when we are married."

Rose laughed as they emerged out into the bright, snow-filled bailey. "I would not want you to be bruised and bleeding, either," she said. Then, she sobered as she gazed up at him, great longing in her expression. "Tell me it will always be like this, James."

He looked at her. "Like what?"

She shrugged, clinging to his hand. "That we will always

laugh with one another," she said. "That we will always have these feelings for one another. I will love you until I die and I never want to feel any differently."

He paused, gazing down into her young, sweet face. "You will never feel any differently," he assured her softly. "Nor will I. I will love you until I die and beyond. You must remember that. You are *my* Rose and always will be."

A smile creased her lips as she smiled. James lifted her hands, kissing them tenderly, but was prevented from doing anything more when a commotion at the gatehouse caught his attention. It seemed that his brothers and cousins had, indeed, returned, bringing not one priest with them but two.

After that, the inhabitants of Castle Questing seemed to fly into a frenzy, for a wedding was swiftly approaching now that the officiants had finally arrived.

It would be the most wonderful Christmas ever.

PART THREE

THE RETURNING

T ROY DE WOLFE had to dodge his eldest son when he entered the bailey; the young man was on a brand new horse he'd been given for Christmas, a young and spirited animal, and he still hadn't figured out how to control the beast. As Troy watched, Andreas struggled with the very strong young colt until the horse reared up and pitched his son into the snow.

Laughter rose up among the men in the bailey as Andreas picked himself up out of a soft snow drift, nothing harmed but his pride. Troy simply shook his head at his sheepish son as he drew his own steed to a halt, dismounting stiffly. His father, William, approached him.

"I must say, I am surprised to see that you made it back so soon," William said. "I can only imagine how bad the roads are with this snow."

Troy nodded his head wearily. In fact, he was exhausted. He leaned against his horse as he pulled off his helm.

"Bad enough," he said. "Fortunately, the road is mostly straight and flat, all the way to Kelso, but the snow was deep and so was the mud."

William could see that. The horse's legs were muddy almost all the way to the shoulder. "Well," he said, slapping the horse on the neck affectionately, "you have returned and that is all that matters. James and Rose are most anxious to wed."

Troy nodded, propping his helm on his saddle. "I know," he said. "We brought Father Bernardo and Father Stephen with us. You know them both, Papa."

William looked over at the two heavily-robed priests as they were helped from the small cart they had been riding on. "I do," he said. "I should go and greet them. And you should take the horse into the stable and warm up his legs. The beast looks like he got the worst of it."

Troy nodded, looking at the mudline on his horse's legs. "Just so you know, Papa," he said before his father could move away, "I will be heading back to Monteviot on the morrow. I do not want to be away from Rhoswyn and the baby much longer, and Patrick will be returning to Berwick tomorrow, also."

Troy and his wife, Rhoswyn, had their first child earlier in the year. With the heavy snows and bad weather, Troy didn't want his wife and infant son to travel to Questing for the wedding, so he'd left them safely at his outpost of Monteviot Tower. Patrick, too, had left his wife at Berwick as she had just delivered a healthy daughter, so both men were without their wives and children. William knew what it was like for a man to be away from his family for any length of time, so he sympathized completely.

"I know," he said. "We shall have the mass at sunset, and you and Patrick can be on your way tomorrow, early. You will see them on the morrow, lad."

Troy simply nodded and turned back to his horse, and William moved towards the priests only to be intercepted by his son, Patrick. The tallest de Wolfe son, and garrison commander of Berwick Castle, greeted his father with a hand to the shoulder.

"Why are you all wet?" Patrick asked, his handsome face curious. "You'd better not let Mother see you like that."

William pursed his lips wryly. "I am a little wet and, suddenly, everyone becomes a nursemaid," he said. "I was throwing snowballs with the children. *That* is why I am wet, if you must know."

Patrick lifted his dark eyebrows at his petulant father. "As I said... you'd better not let Mother see you like that."

As the big son wandered off to stable his horse, William continued on to the priests that had just disembarked from their cart. He knew the men; Father Bernardo was fairly high ranking at Kelso and he was surprised to see the priest. He knew Father Stephen better, and it was Father Stephen who greeted him amiably.

"My lord," the short, round man said pleasantly. "It is a

happy day, indeed. We are honored to be asked to officiate your son's wedding mass."

William dipped his head in polite greeting. "Thank you for coming," he said. "I know the weather was terrible, but my wife and I are prepared to make a sizable donation for your services."

Father Bernardo spoke before Father Stephen could. "So we have been told," he said, seeming displeased. Father Bernardo was slender and bald, and didn't have much of a friendly manner about him. "What I do not understand is why you and your family could not come to Kelso. Why must we come to Questing?"

William lifted his eyebrows as if the priest had asked a genuinely foolish question. "Because we have dozens of children, wives and men," he said. "I also have guests here for the days of Christmas. It is much simpler to bring two priests to me rather than me to bring dozens of people to you in this terrible weather."

While Father Bernardo simply shrugged and looked away, Father Stephen was more apt to smooth over the situation. "We are honored to be here," he said again. "Mayhap we should discuss the coming ceremony inside? It has been very cold today."

William nodded, sweeping his arm towards the entry to Questing's keep. "Then let us retreat to a warm fire," he said. "My wife would like to join us, I am sure, and I would like you to meet the couple you are to marry."

With that, he took the priests inside, leaving his sons and men to disband the escort. There was a palpable sense of excitement now that the priests had arrived, and the wedding they'd all been waiting for would soon be on the horizon.

"YOU DO NOT seem happy for James," Patrick said to Troy. "In fact, you have been quite depressing the past few days. Whatever is the matter with you?"

It was sunset against a clear winter sky and freezing conditions as Patrick and Troy stood just outside of the keep entry, dressed in their finest. They were waiting for Kevin Hage and Apollo de Norville, young knights who were serving at Questing these days, who were making sure the posts were set for the coming night. They were also waiting for the couple to be married to emerge from the keep, along with a host of guests who were inside waiting for the pair. Then they would then all walk in a group to the entry of the great hall where the mass would be said.

The great hall of Questing, built against the outer wall, had glowing innards, light and warmth filtering out into the deepening night. Smells of the coming feast were heavy in the cold air, making everyone hungry with anticipation.

All was as it should be with the wedding imminent, but Troy hadn't seemed pleased with any of it and Patrick wanted to know why. He and Troy were very close, so his concern was genuine. Although he had a suspicion what it was, he still wanted to hear it from his brother.

"Well?" Patrick said after a moment when he failed to get a response to his question. "What is wrong?"

Troy grunted softly. He'd been avoiding giving an answer, but he knew he couldn't avoid it forever. He knew that Patrick already suspected what was wrong.

"Has it been that obvious?" he finally asked.

Patrick nodded. "To me, it has. And probably to Papa. What ails you, Troy?"

Troy was silent for a moment. It was difficult for him to find the words. "It is the same thing that is always the matter with me when the family gathers," he said quietly.

"And that would be?"

"My other half."

So it was out. Patrick knew that's what his brother's trouble was and it was a sensitive subject for them all, especially for Troy and William. To those two, the missing brother was a deeply painful reality and Patrick was careful in how he proceeded with a conversation they'd had, many times, over the past four years.

"He was invited to the wedding," he said quietly. "It was not as if he was excluded. He *was* invited."

"But he did not come."

Patrick scratched at his chin, thinking on what to say. This was something they'd discussed a good deal during Scott's absence and Patrick honestly wasn't sure there was anything more he could say that would be of comfort to Troy.

"Everyone deals with grief in their own way," he finally said. "You know that Scott's way of dealing with it was to run from it. He has started a new life elsewhere and, according to Papa, has finally found peace. Maybe he is simply afraid to come back here to face memories he has tried so hard to forget. You cannot be angry at him for it."

Troy knew all of that. But it wasn't a good excuse, at least not one he was willing to accept.

"Why can he not face it?" he asked. "I went through it, too, you know. Did he think he was the only one to feel that kind of grief? Did he think he was alone in all of it? Of course he wasn't. But instead of facing it, he ran like a coward."

"He was not a coward. He ran because that was his way of dealing with it."

"He ran when I needed him the very most." Troy turned away from his brother, agitated. Talk of his twin truly aggravated him these days; the more time passed, the angrier he became. "I used to feel sorry for him. I used to weep for him and pray he would return, but now… now, I realize he is sending us all a message. Did you ever think of that, Atty? He simply does not wish to have anything to do with us. He does not want to be a de Wolfe any longer."

Atty was the nickname the family called Patrick, something from his childhood. A sweet and endearing name, brother to brother. Patrick could feel Troy's hurt.

"I do not think that is true," he said. "He will come back when he is ready."

Troy whirled to him. "Then let him come," he said, "but I have decided something – I will not welcome him. I have decided that Scott has made a conscious choice not to be my brother any longer."

"That is *not* true."

"Aye, it is. If he cared, he would be here. But he is not. That, my dear brother, is a statement to us all. He would rather not have a family."

Patrick wasn't sure how to respond. He'd seen Troy go from grief-stricken about the entire affair, to patient, to hopeful, and finally to resentment. The entire family had seen the progression and it was something very concerning, especially to William and Jordan. They couldn't have one son hating another and believing the worst, but Troy was heading in that direction very quickly.

Hatred.

It was heartbreaking to watch.

"You know," Patrick said thoughtfully, "you could always go and see him. He is only in Cumbria."

Troy shook his head firmly. "Nay," he said flatly. "*He* left me. I am not going to follow the man around like a lost puppy. If he wants to come to me, then he knows where I am. But he does not want to come. The sooner I get that through my skull, the better I'll be. The better we'll *all* be."

Patrick put his hand on Troy's shoulder. "I think you need to be patient a little longer," he said. "Clearly, Scott is not as strong as you when it comes to dealing with his grief. You must have pity for a man who would run from everything he knows, trying to find a measure of peace. You cannot hate him for it."

Troy just stood there, looking at his shoes and wringing his hands together, trying to warm them in the freezing temperatures. But it was also a nervous tick; he was so very hurt by his twin's behavior over the years, a man he'd been closest to in life. He always thought he knew Scott better than he knew himself, but the deaths of their wives had seen that change drastically. The ironclad bond they'd always shared had rusted and fractured.

The truth was that Troy only felt like a half a man these days. He was devastated to realize that he'd feel like that for the rest of his life.

"Whatever happens, Scott has done it to himself," he said quietly, struggling to calm his anger because he could see people gathering at the keep door. He didn't want them to see him as an emotional mess. "I had no hand in it. Do me a favor, Atty."

"What is it?"

"Do not speak his name to me ever again. Will you do this?"

Patrick felt a great deal of sorrow at that request. "Troy…"

"Please, Atty. Never again. I… cannot…."

It was a plea. Patrick was wise enough to recognize that. Not only had Troy lost his wife in that accident, but he'd also lost his twin. For all intents and purposes, they were both dead to him and he was still trying to work through the pain of it all.

Reaching out, Patrick put a hand on Troy's shoulder.

"If you wish it," he whispered. "But know this… I will never leave you, Troy. I will never run from you. I will always be here for you, no matter what."

Troy looked at his brother, younger by eighteen months, and he forced a smile. Unable to reply for the lump in his throat, he simply coughed, clearing his throat and struggling to regain his composure as people began to spill through the open door of the keep, heading towards the warm and festive great hall. Troy and Patrick stood back as guests and family spilled forth in great, colorful groups.

First came Paris and Caladora, and their children. Paris already had a cup of warmed wine in his hand, something he was loathed to surrender even though his wife had asked him to. He drank it in complete defiance of his wife's wishes. Behind the parents, Hector, Apollo, and Adonis came forth with their respective wives, followed by the youngest de Norville daughter, Cassiopeia, holding hands with Penelope de Wolfe.

As Penelope walked by her older brothers, Patrick reached out and tugged on her braid, causing the girl to shriek angrily. When she looked at him accusingly, he pointed to Troy, who held up a fist as if daring the girl to fight him. In a snit, Penelope turned her nose up at him and marched off.

Grinning at each other for having successfully harassed their baby sister, Troy and Patrick continued to stand there as the de Wolfe family emerged. It was William and Jordan leading most of their offspring, including the younger brothers, Edward and Thomas, and daughter Katheryn, who was married to Alec Hage. Behind the de Wolfe family came a variety of guests, including the Earl of Teviot, Adam de Longley, and his wife, several knights serving de Longley, and several other men who were allied knights of de Longley and de Wolfe.

It was quite a parade of well-dressed, important people, but the Hage family was last, bringing the bride and groom with them. Kieran had hold of Rose, possessively, while James came along behind them, looking rather left out as Kieran and Jemma fussed over their daughter. As James passed by Troy and Patrick, they fell in on either side of him, essentially escorting their brother to his wedding.

Father Bernardo and Father Stephen were waiting for the wedding party at the entrance to the great hall, standing in the arched doorway to begin the mass. Usually, marriages were performed at the doorway to the church but, in this case, it would have to be the great hall. As Rose and James took their places in front of the priests to receive the blessing and have the ceremonial ribbon to bind their hands together, everyone watched with approval and with awe, witnessing the marriage of a couple who were very much in love.

It was a beautiful, touching ceremony from the start.

In the midst of the droning Latin and the ringing of small bells, Troy and Patrick caught a glimpse of their parents up at the front of the crowd; Jordan was weeping with joy while William had a tight hold of Penelope, clinging to his youngest child as he watched James get married. It seemed to Troy that his father needed something to hold on to as another de Wolfe child left the nest. God help them all when Penelope married. But it also made Troy reflect back on the day he married his first wife, Helene, because it was in a group much like this one.

Warm memories enveloped him as he thought back to that balmy summer's day. It had been the first marriage in both families and Paris had wept uncontrollably through the entire ceremony, losing his daughter as he was. Troy grinned to himself as he remembered Helene, usually a cool and calm character, telling her father to stop weeping like a woman. When he wouldn't stop, she started weeping, too. Because she was weeping, her mother and sisters started weeping until there wasn't a dry eye in the church.

Troy still laughed about that.

He was so caught up in his reflections of that bittersweet day that before he realized it, the ceremony was over and everyone was moving into the great hall where a vast feast awaited them. With the wedding concluded, the festivities were beginning and Troy was the last one behind Patrick to filter into the great hall.

As soon as he walked in the door, however, Penelope was standing just inside the doorway with a piece of kindling she'd taken from the hearth. As Patrick stepped through, she whacked the man on the knee, causing him to falter. Troy was swift enough to miss the kindling that came flying at him, which he grabbed and turned on Penelope. But Penelope screamed and ran to her father, pointing out that Troy was trying to beat her with a stick, much to William's disapproval.

So much for Troy and Patrick having the last laugh.

As Penelope smirked, Troy and Patrick plotted their revenge on an eight-year-old girl. But it would have to wait until a time she would least expect it. At the moment, she was on her guard, so Troy and his brother retreated to the long feasting table that contained the newly married couple and most of the families. All was happy and bright as the food began to make its rounds and the wine flowed freely.

The fare for the wedding feast was quite extensive – sides of aged, dried beef had been roasted or boiled, along with fowl, winter vegetables, oat cakes with honey, and a variety of nuts, peas, beans, and copious amounts of bread. It was truly a feast for a king and several of Questing's soldiers, who happened to play instruments, formed a minstrel group in one corner of the hall and began to play loudly.

It was smoky, loud, and warm in the feasting hall as James and Rose were repeatedly toasted. As more good wishes went around the hall, Hector, Apollo, and Alec Hage made their way down the table to sit with Troy and Patrick, senior knights and commanders who had grown up together and had faced both life and death together. The men toasted the married couple, coming up with more toasts as they went along. Very quickly, there was some drunken laughter going on as the expensive and sweet wine flooded their veins.

It was truly an evening to remember.

Troy had forgotten about his absent twin, instead, enjoying the camaraderie that he did have – his brothers, his dear friends and cousins. There were many of them, men he loved dearly, and thoughts of Scott faded as the hours passed. He was more interested in listening to Hector and Apollo, very humorous men, tell stories about their adventure in a seedier part of London when they'd gone there on business with their father. Something about a whore with no hand who used her stump in ways better left unsaid, as Hector explained it, but Apollo swore she was very good with that stump. It was all quite funny and Troy laughed more than he'd laughed in a very long time. He was moderately drunk, and enjoying himself quite a bit, when he looked down the table and caught the expression on his father's face.

As if the man had seen a ghost.

Suddenly, things weren't so funny and Troy was concerned with his father's expression. William was looking at the hall entry, but Troy had his back to it. He was about to turn and look to see what had his father so rattled when his mother suddenly screamed and leapt out of her seat, rushing around the table towards the entry door.

In fact, several people were gasping with surprise, with shock, and James and William actually bolted to their feet. It was then that Troy turned to see what had them all so excited.

It was a sight he never thought he'd see ever again.

"Scott," Troy heard Patrick whisper.

Scott!

Troy could hardly believe his eyes. Was the wine playing tricks on him? He closed his eyes and shook his head, but when he opened his eyes again, Scott de Wolfe was still standing in the hall entry, bundled up heavily against the freezing temperatures.

It was really him.

When Troy realized it was no apparition, he felt as if he'd been hit in the stomach. For a moment, he couldn't breathe. All he could do was stare. Patrick was already out of his seat, moving to the hall entry just as the rest of the de Wolfe family was, and Troy could hear his mother weeping as she threw her arms around her Prodigal Son.

God, they were painful tears, tears of joy and yet sorrow. Four years of longing, of waiting and wondering, had finally come to an end for Jordan and all of the emotion she'd kept bottled up for those years was bursting forth.

Scott had come home!

The joy, the surprise, was contagious. The entire table began gravitating in Scott's direction at this point, everyone moving to greet the son that had run off those years ago. Troy actually lost sight of Scott as the man was bombarded by people who were so very happy to see him, so anxious to greet him.

All except Troy.

He was virtually the only one left at the table because he simply couldn't make himself go to the man. As shocked as he was to see him, it was shock compounded with all of the bitterness and resentment he'd been feeling. Those emotions were always close to the surface when it came to Scott. But now with the man's surprising appearance, they were stronger than they'd ever been.

All he could feel now was loathing.

And he wasn't going to go running to the man and welcome him back, pretending that everything was all right, pretending that Scott hadn't hurt people with his cowardice. When he'd run out, he'd taken the guts of his parents and everyone else who loved him and stomped on them. Now, here he was, returned because he received an invitation to his brother's wedding. Or was it something else?

Was he here to ruin Christmas for them all?

Well, Troy wasn't going to put up with it. He simply turned around, collected his cup of wine, and pretended not to care. But that wasn't good enough. He could still hear people welcoming Scott. Everyone was so happy about it. He could hear his Uncle Paris's voice above all. The man was ecstatic. That kind of joy sickened and disgusted Troy. Didn't they remember what Scott had done to them all?

Didn't they realize he had made a conscious choice not to be part of the family?

But Troy realized it. He realized what everyone else did not. Slamming his cup down, he vacated the table and slipped out of the hall from the servant's alcove.

Out in the crisp, black night, he moved away from the hall and the festivities, struggling to get a rein on his emotions. He wasn't paying attention to where he was going; he was simply walking, putting distance between himself and the great hall where his Prodigal Brother had returned. He didn't want to see him; he *couldn't* see him. All of those people were gleefully willing to forget Scott's selfishness, but Troy wasn't.

He wasn't willing to forget anything.

Somehow, Troy found himself in Questing's long, slender chapel. The front half of the structure was the church while the back half of it was a burial crypt. Scott's wife, Athena, and their two children, Beatrice and Andrew, were buried there, right next to Helene and her two children, Arista and Acacia. The women were lying head to head in their separate crypts, close in death as they had been in life.

Troy wandered into the rear of the chapel, going to Helene's crypt, which was something he did every time he visited Questing. His new wife, Rhoswyn, had visited Helene, too, so it wasn't unusual for Troy to be here. These days, he felt peace with it, like visiting an old friend. But now, he was here to talk to the dead. He didn't want to talk to anyone living at the moment.

They wouldn't understand.

Helene's crypt had a beautifully carved effigy of her holding her two daughters in slumber and at her feet lay a wolf. Carved into the base of the crypt were the following words –

Lady Helene, beloved wife of Troy

Arista – Acacia

They are simply sleeping

Troy stood there a moment, looking at the effigy of his first wife. He had been here for her, even after death. He'd respected her memory, unlike his brother. Then, his gaze moved to Athena's crypt and he wandered over to it. Her effigy was nearly the same, only she had her two children on either side of her, arms around them both. At the base of her crypt was inscribed:

Lady Athena, beloved wife of Scott

Andrew – Beatrice

Angels on earth, angels in heaven

Troy sighed heavily as he looked at his sister-in-law's crypt. The more he looked at it, the more angst he felt.

"He's returned, Tee," he said quietly. "Can you believe it? I just saw him standing in the great hall. James has married, you know. I do not know if your mother or father have told you, but James married Rosie today. The entire family was here except Scott, but he just showed up. Everyone is welcoming him home as if he is a long-lost hero."

Even as he said it, he could hear his bitterness in his voice. So much anger. He put his hands on Athena's crypt, distress in his expression.

"I never told you how sorry I was for what he did," he said hoarsely. "When you and Bee and Andy were brought back, someone should have been there for you. *Scott* should have been there for you. He was your husband, was he not? But he left you to die alone, to be buried alone. He left it to the rest of us to try to fill that hole, but we could not. Scott was such a coward that he ran away and left everything behind. Now, he has come back and I do not know what to do. I am not sure I can overcome what he's done."

Those last few words were the crux of the situation. Too much sadness and resentment had built up in Troy for him to adequately handle what he was feeling. He moved to stand between the two crypts, leaning against Helene's crypt as he put his hand on the head of Athena's effigy.

"I have gone my entire life believing my brother was the most noble, moral man alive," he muttered. "He could do no wrong in my eyes. He was perfect and I adored him. But when he ran… that made me see him differently. That made me see how weak he truly was and, try as I might, I am still having trouble accepting that the man I loved most in this world, the man I thought I knew better than anyone, is a coward. Is that to be his legacy? That he ran away when you and the children needed him most?"

"Do you want to know why I ran away?"

A familiar voice filled the dark, musty air of the burial vault and Troy turned to see Scott standing just inside the doorway that led from the nave.

For a moment, Troy simply stood there and stared at the man, a million thoughts and emotions running through his mind. But he couldn't seem to grasp one, nor speak one. He couldn't seem to bring forth those words of hatred or condemnation when he needed them most. But as he looked at his brother, the wall of composure he'd kept up was starting to come down, stone by stone. He could feel the angst in his chest bursting forth and it was difficult... so very difficult... to keep a rein on what he was feeling.

"What are you doing here?" he finally asked. "How did you find me?"

"Papa thought you might have come here."

Troy grunted, returning his gaze to the crypt. "And so, I did," he said. "I never thought I would see you ever again."

Scott de Wolfe took a step into the vault, and then another. Whereas Troy was dark-haired and rather swarthy looking, Scott took after their mother's side of the family, with honey-blond hair and hazel eyes. He was riveted to his twin, a man he hadn't seen in four years and, suddenly, four years of longing and pain and confusion seemed to come to a rapid head. Seeing his brother was emotional enough, but seeing the contempt in his brother's eyes was more than his soul could bear. At this moment, at this blessed moment, Scott had to say what he'd been waiting four years to say, whether or not Troy wanted to hear it.

He'd come all this way to say it.

"I can imagine that you thought so," he said huskily. "I am equally sure that you are not anxious to do so. I do not blame you, Troy. I do not fault you for anything you are feeling towards me. But for my own sake, I must tell you why I ran that day."

Troy was starting to tremble, his emotions getting the better of him. He pointed to Athena's effigy. "Do not tell me," he said. "Tell *her*. Tell Tee why you ran off like a coward instead of remaining with her like you should have. The woman had to be buried alone, for Christ's sake, because her husband was nowhere to be found. Do you have any idea how horrible that was?"

Behind him, he could hear Scott's footfalls as the man made his way over to the crypt that contained his dead wife and children. They were slow and labored steps. Finally, Scott just stood there a moment, staring down at the crypt, and Troy couldn't even look at him. He had to turn away, realizing his eyes were burning with angry, unshed tears.

"Greetings, Tee," Scott said softly, although his voice was tight with emotion. "I am sure you do not wish to see me, either, but I have come nonetheless. Troy is right... you were buried alone. I should have been here for you and the children, but I was not. God forgive me for that. But something caused me to run, something that affected me so deeply that it was as if I no longer had any control over my heart or my mind. Troy has asked me to tell you why I ran away when I should have remained here, strong and tall, so I will tell you. I remember that day very clearly, you see, because I had spoken with you right before you got into that carriage with your sister. Do you recall? I was the one who had the carriage brought around and I was the one who personally loaded you and Bea and Andy into the carriage. I kissed you farewell and I watched you ride off, knowing full well that we'd had terrible rains as of late and that the rivers and creeks between Questing and Berwick Castle were overflowing their banks. You were going to Berwick that day to see Patrick's new son. I even loaded the baby's gifts into the carriage with you. *I put you in that carriage.*"

There was no reply from the stone effigy. Not that Scott expected that there would be, but after four years of avoiding this moment, now he was here, facing his dead wife and children, feeling those emotions of grief and anguish bubble up again, emotions he had healed from for the most part. But he knew he would never be completely healed until he faced what terrified him most, and this was that moment.

He was facing the results of his actions.

"It was me," he said as he began to break down. "*I did it. I put you and Helene in the carriage. I could have stopped you; I could have told you to travel another day when the land was not so soggy, but I did not. I was preoccupied with an errand for my father and I was not as cautious as I should have been. All of this... you and the children, Helene and the girls... all of this was because of me.*"

His voice cracked at the end and the tears began to fall on the stone. Standing at the head of the crypt, Troy couldn't stop the tears, either. Hearing his brother's voice, hearing his thoughts and emotions from the past four years, were carving into him like a knife. The pain was excruciating. He was still looking away from Scott, his eyes closed as tears streamed down his cheeks.

So, the truth had come forth – the guilt Scott had felt at

letting the women go on the journey that would ultimately claim their lives. It had never even crossed Troy's mind that Scott should feel that way, for what had happened had been an accident. At least, Troy saw it that way, but Scott had clearly spent four years shouldering tremendous guilt.

God, it was horrific to hear.

"Scott…," he began hoarsely.

But Scott cut him off. "I am sorry, Troy," he wept softly. "I am so sorry that I caused your pain. I am so sorry that I did this to you. If I could have exchanged my life for the lives of Athena and Helene, please know that I would have. But the worst part of all was when I returned to Questing and Papa told me what had happened. As I stood there, unable to believe it, you came out of the keep and fell to your knees. As I watched, the strongest man I'd ever known vomited into the earth and collapsed right before my very eyes. And I watched it all, knowing that it was my fault. Your pain was *my* fault. Was I a coward for running? I was. God knows, I was. But I was too disturbed to stay, too afraid I would crumble into a thousand pieces of agony that would never be put back together again. If grief had collapsed you the way it did, what on earth would it do to me?"

Troy had his hand over his face, weeping into his hand. It was the grieving he'd done four years ago, now with his brother's pain compounding his because Scott felt that he was to blame for everything.

Now, he was grieving for his brother.

"It was *not* your fault," Troy whispered, wiping at his face and struggling to stop the tears. Finally, he looked at his brother, seeing the man he'd always loved, the man he'd been the closest to. "I never blamed you for what happened. But I did blame you for running from it."

"I could not face you."

"What else was I supposed to think, if not cowardice, from a man who did not have a cowardly bone in his body? How was I supposed to know you ran because of guilt?"

Scott shook his head, not even bothering to wipe the tears from his face. "You could not think anything other than what you did," he said. "It looks like cowardice. It *was*. But in my defense, I saw it as self-preservation, I suppose. I saw it as removing the cause of everyone's anguish."

Troy took a deep breath, fighting down the tears and struggling for calm. All of the anger and resentment he'd been feeling was melting away as he began to understand Scott's perspective.

In truth, he should have suspected it all along, but he'd been too hurt to try. Now, he understood a great deal and the hate, the bitterness, was gone. He couldn't keep it up, not when Scott was hurting so badly. He went to his brother, a man he loved so deeply, and put his hand on the man's face. He just stood there a moment, looking at him, feeling as if all of this was some kind of dream. Scott was really here, in front of him, and it was time for him to say everything he'd been wanting to say to the man.

He'd waited long enough.

"It was *not* your fault," he said, more firmly. "It was a terrible accident. It could have been any one of us putting the women in the carriage and seeing them off. It just happened to be you. And it never occurred to me, in all these four years, to blame you for that. I do not, nor have I ever, blamed you for what happened. But I have missed you every single day of the past four years, Scott. I thought you decided you did not want to be my brother any longer."

Scott smiled weakly, seeing the light of forgiveness in his brother's eyes where only moments before, there had been animosity and rage. "I thought, mayhap, you did not want *me* to be your brother any longer," he admitted.

Troy shook his head. "You are part of me and I am part of you," he said. "But I am sorry you felt as if you had to stay away. I am sorry you did not feel as if we could draw strength from one another in this time of sorrow."

Scott reached up, gripping the hand that was on his face. His brother's touch was incredibly comforting, more than he'd ever realized. "I was a fool," he said. "It took me a long time to come to terms with my grief and with my guilt. It was just easier to try and shut everything out so it did not consume me. The longer I stayed away, the more difficult it was to face it."

Troy understood that. Sometimes, men had moments of weakness that they lived to regret. He gripped his brother's hand tightly.

"Tell me that you will not disappear again, then," he said.

"Tell me that you have come home to stay and that we shall never again be without each other."

Scott was nodding his head even before Troy finished his sentence. "That is why I came home," he said. "It was time. When I received the missive regarding James' wedding, I knew I had to come. My wife encouraged me to come."

Troy smiled faintly. "Papa said you had married again."

Scott smiled in return. "Avrielle is her name," he said. "She is a remarkable woman of great wisdom and I considered myself blessed. You will like her, Troy. I know you will."

"I am sure of it."

"Papa tells me that you have married again, too."

Troy nodded. "Rhoswyn is Scots," he said. "A finer woman you will never meet."

"Papa also says she terrorizes you."

Troy broke down into a laugh. "When you meet her, see if she does not terrorize you, also," he said. "She is the only child of Red Keith Kerr and he raised her like a son. She fights like a warrior, Scott. Do not tangle with the woman, for you will lose."

Scott was warming to the conversation, so incredibly glad to be speaking to his brother again, as if he'd never left him. The warmth, the bond, was still there. It hadn't been completely destroyed, and he could feel it strengthening by the second.

"Red Keith Kerr, you say?" he repeated. "Of Sibbald's Hold?"

"The same."

"I did not even know he had a daughter."

"Nor did I until it was too late."

Scott laughed. Troy laughed. Suddenly, they were throwing their arms around each other, embracing one another tightly. All of the hurt, guilt, and resentment was gone in that instant, never to come between them again.

"God, I've missed you," Troy said, his throat tight with emotion. "Swear to me you will not leave me again. When you left, I felt so abandoned."

Scott clutched his brother tightly. "I swear I will never leave you, not ever," he whispered. "Forgive me for leaving you, Troy. Forgive me for not being strong enough to stay."

Troy stopped hugging his brother long enough to look the man in the eye. "You did what you had to do in order to keep your sanity," he said. "I suppose I understand that now. Everyone was trying to tell me that, but it was difficult to swallow. But as Papa has said all along, every man grieves in his own way. My way was to remain here and to suffer through the agony. Your way was to try to forget about it. But I am so sorry you felt as if you were responsible for everything. It was not your fault."

Scott forced a smile at his beloved brother. "I will come to accept that someday."

Troy patted him on the cheek again. "I hope you do," he said. "Now... I suppose we should go back to the hall. Everyone will want to see you, you know. Already, it is probably killing Mother to give us this time alone."

Scott's grin broadened. "Papa is probably having to tie her down somewhere."

Troy snorted. "Then we had better go back to the hall and spare them both the agony."

Scott nodded, but his gaze moved to the crypt containing his wife and younger children. "Go ahead," he said. "I need to spend a few moments with Tee and the girls, as I should have done before."

That gave Troy pause. "Will you be okay?"

"I will, I swear it."

"As you wish," Troy said. His eyes lingered on the man for a moment. "I am so glad you've come home. It is the best Christmas gift I could have hoped for."

Scott gave him a lopsided grin. "A Christmas miracle is more like it. The miracle is your forgiveness, Troy."

Troy simply shook his head. "It is the bond of brotherhood that goes deeper than any common bond," he said. "Whatever happened four years ago… remember that we are stronger together than apart."

"Agreed."

Giving his brother another hug, Troy wandered from the vault, leaving Scott alone in the shadowed, cold depths. Once he heard Troy's boot falls fade, he turned to the beautiful effigy of the woman he once loved.

Reaching out, he put a hand on her cold, stone face.

"Mayhap if Troy can forgive me, you can, too," he murmured. "Mayhap someday, I will feel as if you have. But I do want to tell you that I have remarried, Tee. I know you would like her – she is kind and generous, and I love her. I never thought I would find love again, but I have. I hope – nay, I *know* – that you are happy for me."

It made him think of Avrielle, his wife, and all of his children, both living and dead. He'd suffered through some terrible tragedies in his life, but he was home again now. He would be stronger for it. Reaching out, he touched the effigy one last time.

"I thought you would want to know that I am happy again," he whispered. "I hope you are, too."

There was no answer, of course, but Scott smiled at the effigy just the same. He'd been dreading this moment, the moment when he would face his wife's crypt. But it was becoming easier as the moments passed. He was coming to grips with it and he knew it wouldn't be the last time he came to visit Athena and the children. In fact, returning to Castle Questing felt as if he'd never left. Wherever he lived, Questing would always be home to him. As much as he loved his new wife and his life with her in the wilds of Cumbria, Questing was where his family was.

As difficult as it had been, he was glad he'd come home.

Very glad.

Bending over the crypt, he kissed Athena, Beatrice, and Andrew's effigies, feeling that some larger part of him was now complete. No more guilt, no more missing his family, no more trying to shut out a part of his life that could not be forgotten.

He didn't want to forget about it any longer.

Someday, he'd bring Avrielle to Questing and then, the healing process would be complete. He would come full circle. But until that time, he intended to enjoy the family he'd not seen in four long years.

Finally, the Prodigal Son had returned. Peace had been made.

On a dark and cold December night, the de Wolfes had the most joyous Christmas of all.

THE END

A Joyous de Wolfe Christmas is an extended epilogue for ShadowWolfe and DarkWolfe.

About Kathryn Le Veque

Medieval Just Got Real.

KATHRYN LE VEQUE is a USA TODAY Bestselling author, an Amazon All-Star author, and a #1 bestselling, award-winning, multi-published author in Medieval Historical Romance and Historical Fiction. She has been featured in the NEW YORK TIMES and on USA TODAY's HEA blog. In March 2015, Kathryn was the featured cover story for the March issue of InD'Tale Magazine, the premier Indie author magazine. She was also a quadruple nominee (a record!) for the prestigious RONE awards for 2015.

Kathryn's Medieval Romance novels have been called 'detailed', 'highly romantic', and 'character-rich'. She crafts great adventures of love, battles, passion, and romance in the High Middle Ages. More than that, she writes for both women AND men – an unusual crossover for a romance author – and Kathryn has many male readers who enjoy her stories because of the male perspective, the action, and the adventure.

On October 29, 2015, Amazon launched Kathryn's Kindle Worlds Fan Fiction site WORLD OF DE WOLFE PACK. Please visit Kindle Worlds for Kathryn Le Veque's World of de Wolfe Pack and find many action-packed adventures written by some of the top authors in their genre using Kathryn's characters from the de Wolfe Pack series. As Kindle World's FIRST Historical Romance fan fiction world, Kathryn Le Veque's World of de Wolfe Pack will contain all of the great story-telling you have come to expect.

Kathryn loves to hear from her readers. Please find Kathryn on Facebook at Kathryn Le Veque, Author, or join her on Twitter @kathrynleveque, and don't forget to visit her website and sign up for her blog at www.kathrynleveque.com.

Please follow Kathryn on Bookbub for the latest releases and sales: bookbub.com/authors/kathryn-le-veque.

Made in the USA
Coppell, TX
09 December 2020

43902250R20039